How to make your ~~...~~ Wishes.

W I S H

With this book comes an extra special wish for you and your best friend.

Hold the book together at each end and both close your eyes.

Wriggle your noses and think of a number under ten.

Open your eyes, whisper the numbers you thought of to each other.

Add these numbers together. This is your

⋆ ⋆ Magic Number ⋆
⋆

you

best friend

Place your little finger on the stars, and say your magic number out loud together. Now make your wish quietly to yourselves. And maybe, one day, your wish might just come true. Love

felicity

x

For my baby niece, Amelia Bo
E.V.T

felicity Wishes®

FELICITY WISHES
Felicity Wishes © 2000 Emma Thomson
Licensed by White Lion Publishing

Text and Illustrations © 2004 Emma Thomson

First published in Great Britain in 2004 by Hodder Children's Books

The right of Emma Thomson to be identified as the author and illustrator of this work has
been asserted by her in accordance with the Copyright, Designs and Patents Act 1988.

2 4 6 8 10 9 7 5 3

A Catalogue record for this book is available from the British Library

ISBN 0 340 88239 5

Printed and bound in Great Britain by Bookmarque Ltd, Croydon, Surrey

The paper and board used in this paperback by Hodder Children's Books are natural recyclable
products made from wood grown in sustainable forests. The manufacturing processes
conform to the environmental regulations of the country of origin.

Hodder Children's Books
A division of Hodder Headline Ltd, 338 Euston Road, London NW1 3BH

CONTENTS

Cinema Collision

Polly had been waiting for Felicity Wishes to answer her front door for ages. When she bent over and peeped through the letterbox, she couldn't believe her eyes. "What in fairy world are you doing?" she called through the flap.

"Just coming!" strained Felicity, sounding panicky.

When Felicity did finally open her door it was with her foot! Her arms were tied up in so much wool it had proved impossible to free herself completely.

Polly stood silently on the doorstep, dumbfounded.

"Come in, won't you?" said Felicity, pogoing ahead of her. "I had a bit of an accident, but I'm sorting it out now."

"What...?" was all Polly could say, when she saw the mountain of wool in Felicity's sitting room.

"I don't know what went wrong," said Felicity, trying to free her arms. "Would you like to get yourself a drink... sorry to be a terrible host. I'd get you one myself only..."

"Only you're a bit tied up!" said Polly, suddenly bursting out into fits of giggles. "Oh, Felicity! What are you like? If you tell me where I can

find some scissors, I can help get you
out of this mess!"

Felicity pointed with her best ballet
foot to the drawer in the large gold
cupboard in the corner.

* * *

Soon Felicity was free and the two of them were sitting around the kitchen table drinking strawberry milkshakes.

"I've just been so bored!" confided Felicity to her friend, "and it's only the first week of the holidays."

"Why don't you tidy your bedroom?" suggested Polly, who was always very practical.

"What's the point when it just gets messy again," said Felicity, slurping froth through her straw noisily.

"What about gardening? Why don't you plant some bulbs and tend to them as they grow?" said Polly.

Felicity dropped her straw. "You know I'm not like Daisy. I don't like getting my wand dirty, and there are always all those creepy-crawlies."

"What about taking up a hobby, maybe making something?" suggested Polly, undeterred.

"You mean like knitting?" said Felicity, pulling several strands of wool from her hair.

"Maybe not," said Polly giggling, and reached over to pick up *The Daily Flutter* from the pile of magazines for inspiration.

"I know!" she said, turning to the back page and pointing. "Why don't you get a holiday job?"

"A job?" said Felicity frowning. "That doesn't sound like much fun to me."

"It could be doing anything though," said Polly, getting quite excited herself. "If I wasn't busy writing a book about teeth, I'd get a job during the holidays."

11

Polly wanted to be a Tooth Fairy. She was the most studious of all Felicity's friends and had set herself the task of writing a book about her favourite subject in her time off.

"Look!" she continued. "There's all sorts. Cinema Attendants, Waitresses, Temporary Post Fairy positions, there's even a vacancy for a Dental Assistant," Polly said dreamily.

"Let me see," said Felicity, turning the paper to face her. "Hmm, cinema attendants give out ice-cream, don't they?" she said thoughtfully, "...and they get to watch the latest films all day!" she continued, her mind racing, "...and the only bit that could get boring would be showing people to their seats."

"But that's not boring," said Polly, trying to encourage her friend. "Just think of all the fairies you could meet, and all the friends you could make!"

That did it! Felicity's favourite
thing in the whole world was making
friends and she was known as being
one of the friendliest fairies in Little
Blossoming. The job of cinema
attendant sounded perfect!

Without losing any time, Felicity
carefully tore out the advert, picked
up her wand and flew with Polly
straight down to
the cinema.

When she emerged
from the cinema, Felicity was
bouncing for joy!

"I got it!" she squealed, clapping
her hands. "I got the job, and I start
right away!"

"That's fantastic," said Polly, who
had been waiting anxiously for her
friend. "Why don't we meet at
Sparkles when you're finished and
you can tell me all about it!"

"OK – see you later," called Felicity as she disappeared off to put on her new uniform.

* * *

Polly had arranged for Felicity's two other close friends, Holly and Daisy, to be in Sparkles, the café, when she finished the first day at her new job.

Holly spotted Felicity first and waved her wand frantically to catch her attention.

"Over here!" she called.

Felicity, head down, walked slowly towards their table.

"How did it go?" said Daisy excitedly. "Polly told us all about it! It sounds wonderful."

"Wonderful if you like scary monsters," said Felicity as she sat down.

"What do you mean?" said Polly, confused. "I thought you were handing out ice-creams in the cinema and showing fairies to their seats."

Felicity picked up her hot chocolate to steady her shaking hands and only succeeded in spilling it all over the table. She burst into tears.

"Oh, I can't do anything right," she said.

Polly got up and gave her a hug. "Tell us all about it," she said softly.

"Everything began so magically," Felicity said, wiping away her tears. "My uniform was pink and white striped, which I was very happy about because it matched my favourite tights, and then they gave me the most enormous box of yummy ice-cream to hang around my neck!"

"It does sound wonderful," said Holly, confused.

"And that wasn't all," continued Felicity. "Soon the whole cinema was full of fairies who were so nice."

"What happened?" said Daisy, putting down her mug.

"Well, I was so busy chatting and making friends, the film had already started by the time I got round to showing the fairies to their seats. It was dark, and even with my torch I kept tripping up. So did the fairies who'd come to see the film. There was popcorn and fizzy pop everywhere!"

"It's an easy mistake," said Polly, rubbing Felicity's arm. "It was dark."

"That's just what the manageress said when she heard all the commotion," continued Felicity, "which made me feel a bit better. But not for long. The film showing was a horror film, with big scary monsters. I couldn't look at the screen, and so instead I ended up staring at the ice-cream hanging around my neck. It looked so nice, and I thought it was probably important that I knew what all the flavours tasted like."

"You didn't eat it all?!" said Holly, clamping her hand over her mouth.

"I didn't mean to," said Felicity. "But somehow it just happened. There was none left in the interval for anyone else and everybody got very upset."

"Well, it's not a disaster, it was just your first day. I'm sure the manageress understood that it was really just a mistake."

"Well, no," said Felicity sheepishly. "It probably would have been OK. That is, if I hadn't been sick. All over aisle G."

All three of Felicity's fairy friends groaned in despair and buried their faces in their hands.

The fairies finished up their hot chocolates and gave Felicity a lot of fairy hugs and encouragement for finding a new job, then went their separate ways home.

* * *

It was a week before they all met up again to see how Felicity had got on with her job-hunting but she didn't seem any happier.

"Well," began Felicity, looking very sorry for herself. "My job of Post Fairy

started well. The Post Office offered
me a job posting special letters in the
afternoon. My first
day went brilliantly.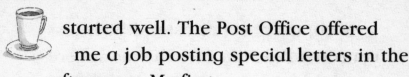
I had five letters and
everyone I delivered them to ended
up inviting me in for a cup of tea.
That day I made five new friends."

"How lovely," said Daisy.

" It was the next day that
everything went a bit wrong,"
continued Felicity. " I had twenty-five
letters to post, and by the end of
the day I had drunk ten cups of tea
and had only posted nine letters."

"Ten teas and nine letters?"
asked Holly, confused.

"Yes, Miss Meandering the
geography teacher had a lovely
letter from a fairy friend in
Russia, and I drank two cups
of tea while she translated
it for me."

"What did you do?" asked Polly, concerned.

"Oh, the post mistress asked me to hand the undelivered letters back and said I should leave. She was very nice but she just didn't think my skills were suited to the job."

"I think you should try something artistic. You're so good at that sort of thing," suggested Daisy.

"Oh, I did that after the Post Fairy job," said Felicity. "I decided to make friendship bracelets for a shop in Bloomfield," and Felicity waggled her hand in front of her friends to show them one of her creations.

"That's lovely!" said Holly, who was always very fashionable. "The colours you've used are beautiful."

"And the detail in the tiny plaits you've woven must have taken ages," said Polly, carefully studying her friend's bracelet.

"We'll all have to go to the shop in Bloomfield to get one," said Daisy, impressed.

Felicity pulled her hand away from her friends' gaze. "Well, there might be a problem with that."

"You can't tell me that they don't like your bracelets" said Holly, astonished.

"No, they love them, they've ordered a hundred," said Felicity. "It's just that, this is the only one I've made so far, and it took me two days, and..." she yawned, "...two nights."

All the fairy friends exchanged helpless glances.

"Perhaps a holiday job wasn't the answer after all," suggested Polly. "Maybe gossiping in Sparkles is the best remedy for being bored in the school holidays." All the fairy friends agreed.

"Anybody want another milkshake?" offered Felicity.

"I'd love a hot chocolate if you're going up to order. They're being a bit slow today," said Polly.

"More carrot cake please," said Holly.

"I ordered a jasmine tea ages ago," said Daisy.

* * *

When Felicity got up to the counter to place the order she found a couple of fairies waiting impatiently. There was no one serving.

Being friendly, it wasn't long before Felicity found herself chatting to the fairies in front of her.

"Look," she suggested, "why don't
you all tell me where you're sitting
and what you want and I'll bring
your orders to you.
It seems silly for all of us to waste
gossiping time waiting!"

The fairies agreed and Felicity
borrowed a notebook and pen
from the counter to write
down everyone's orders.

It wasn't long before a very hot and bothered fairy fluttered frantically from behind the big swing doors that led to the kitchen.

"Sorry to keep you waiting" she puffed, wiping her brow with a red spotty hanky. "We're having a terrible time here. Our head waitress isn't well and we were already short of staff."

"Oh, what a shame," said Felicity. "Can I help? I've just taken the orders for those fairies but I can stay here and keep taking new orders if you'd like."

"Oh, you're an angel fairy! Let me introduce myself: I'm Sally, the owner. The job's yours!" Sally tossed Felicity a white frilly apron. "And you can start immediately!"

Felicity was taken aback. "Job?" she muttered to herself. "I was just being friendly!"

"Right," said Sally, looking down Felicity's list and pouring drinks faster than Felicity had ever seen. "These go to table four in the corner. I'll have the next order ready for you when you get back."

As Felicity quickly tied her apron, took the tray and dashed off towards table four, she found herself heading towards her friends.

"Don't ask!" she laughed at their astonished faces as she dropped off Daisy's jasmine tea, Holly's carrot cake and Polly's hot chocolate. "If only I had known that I didn't have to find my perfect job after all. It just found me!" And all of her fairy friends cheered!

Enjoy today
because tomorrow will bring unexpected surprises

Fashion Passion

"Humpf!" sighed Felicity Wishes, as she dramatically flung herself from one side of her bed to the other in an attempt to get comfortable.

She opened one eye and looked at her pink alarm clock.

"Ohh," she moaned, and pulled the covers over her head.

Felicity had never been one for early mornings. Her holiday job at Sparkles, the café on the corner, had meant that she had had to get up early. Now that the holiday was nearly over and the job had come to an end, she just couldn't help herself from waking up wide-eyed hours before she had to. It was a very frustrating way for a fairy to start her day.

After finally admitting defeat, Felicity threw off her duvet and walked heavily towards her bathroom. By the time she was washed and dressed it was still only 7.30am.

"No one else will be awake for ages," she said to herself as she pulled open her curtains and looked down on Little Blossoming. "What am I going to do with all this time?"

Then suddenly she had a thought. She picked up her wand, flew out the door and headed straight to Sticky Bun the Baker's on the high street. With a large bag full of fresh croissants Felicity set about delivering the delicious breakfast treat to her friends. First stop was Holly's house.

"Morning," sang Felicity as a very sleepy Holly peered round the corner of the door.

"Oh, it's you. I thought it might be the Post Fairy," said Holly, ushering Felicity in. "It's ever so early, are you OK? Has there been an accident?"

"No, no," said Felicity, looking shocked, at her fairy friend's hair.

"Have you had an accident?" and without thinking, she added, "You look dreadful!"

Holly dreamed of being a Christmas Fairy and always prided herself on her appearance. She was rarely seen with one hair out of place – let alone all of them!

Holly scowled. "True beauty takes a lot of careful preparation..." and spotting the bag of croissants Felicity was holding, she smiled, "...that can wait until after breakfast!"

The two fairy friends gossiped happily for so long they didn't notice they had eaten all the croissants.

"Fancy going shopping later?" suggested Holly, brushing the crumbs from her pyjama top.

"I went shopping yesterday, and every day last week," said Felicity glumly. "I never thought I'd hear myself say this, but I'm tired of shopping this holiday. Let's find something new to do!"

"How can you be tired of shopping?!" said Holly, shocked. "What about that new exclusive shop that will only let you in with a member's pass? You can't possibly be tired of that."

"I'm not a member," said Felicity and sighed.

Then Holly had a brilliant thought. "Let's make up our own Fashion Club, where we can all be members!"

Felicity jumped out of her seat. "What a sparkletastic idea!" she squealed. "We can have our own membership cards, and passwords, and everything! We can have a secret headquarters, and we'll research the latest trends and discuss where to find the latest looks, and how to look stylish at all times!"

"Well," said Holly smoothing down her bed head, "nearly all times!"

Holly was so excited about sharing the Fashion Club plans with the rest of their fairy friends that she only took half the time she normally took to do her hair, put on her make-up and get dressed.

* * *

When they arrived on Daisy's doorstep
they were both out of breath. Daisy
wanted to be a Blossom Fairy when
she graduated from the School of
Nine Wishes, and she had spent the
morning carefully selecting petals
from her pressed flower collection to
make into hand-made birthday cards.
Holly and Felicity flew into Daisy's
sitting room with such a flutter,
petals flew everywhere.
"We're going to
start a Fashion
Club!" they
announced
together,
unable to
contain their
excitement.
"What a lovely idea!"
said Daisy, trying to
catch the falling petals
in her skirt. "Flowers, you

know, are always in fashion. Can I be in the club too?"

"Yes, yes!" said Felicity. "You could give talks on floral fabrics, and..."

"...And you could make fashionable flowery badges and membership cards for everyone!" continued Holly, picking up one of Daisy's handmade birthday cards.

"Have you told Polly yet?" asked Daisy. "Because she's always so good at everything, I bet she could make up a brilliant code and password for us to use."

And before the last petal had fallen to the floor, Holly, Felicity and Daisy were on their way to Polly's house to enrol her in their fashion plan.

* * *

All four fairies sat around Polly's kitchen table. Each had a piece of paper on which they had written Fairy Fashion Club Plans at the top.

Felicity had decorated hers with doodles of tiny daisies.

fairy fashion Club plans

- Holly – design club uniform
- Daisy – make club badges and membership cards
- Polly – make up club code and password
- Felicity – find headquarters and enrol new members
? ?

With their plans in place, the fairies decided to split up and meet back at Sparkles later that day with their tasks complete. There wasn't much of the school holiday left and there was no time to lose!

Felicity Wishes was in her element. She was the friendliest fairy in Little Blossoming.

Enrolling new members meant that Felicity could spend her time doing what she loved most, making new friends to be part of the Fairy Fashion Club. First on the agenda though was to find somewhere for them all to meet, and with fluttering wings she set off on her search.

First stop was her bedroom. It had a lovely pink door with a gap just big enough for slipping notes and passwords underneath, and it was right at the top of the house, so they could keep a look-out for any Fashion Club members approaching.

"The only thing it doesn't have," said Felicity to herself, "is space."

If Felicity's bedroom was tidy you could probably squeeze about ten fairies in for a club meeting. But

Felicity's bedroom was rarely tidy and fitting more than four pairs of wings in the room, amongst all the discarded dresses, stripy tights, books and magazines that covered the floor, would be a problem.

Felicity sighed and reluctantly put a big red line through "bedroom" on her list.

Next stop was the school bike sheds. It was big, easy for everyone to get to, and perfect for last minute emergency Fashion Club meetings during break times. As Felicity flew towards the School of Nine Wishes she spotted Holly flying in the opposite direction with two large bags.

"What have you got in there?" she said hovering to chat for a moment.

"Club T-shirts for our uniform. I'm going to customise them with ribbons, buttons and bows to create something so original everyone will want one!"

"They sound perfect!" said Felicity.

"I'm just off to see if the school bike sheds would be OK for our head-quarters."

"Bike sheds?" said Holly, so shocked she nearly forgot to flap her wings.

"Hmm," said Felicity, showing Holly her list.

"My bedroom was a little messy for everyone to fit in."

"I hate to interfere," said Holly, "but bike sheds are very dirty. It's not really a very glamorous address to put on our membership cards."

"I didn't think of that," admitted Felicity sadly.

"I must go – these bags are too

heavy to hover with any more. Good luck with your search, and see you later," and with that Holly was gone.

Quietly Felicity floated to the ground. There was no point in flying to see the bike sheds now. There was nowhere else left on her list of possible headquarters to try. Felicity closed her eyes and put her head in her hands and tried with all her might to think of somewhere else.

Suddenly she felt a tap on her shoulder. "Everything OK?" said Daisy smiling.

"Not really," said Felicity. She noticed the large tube under Daisy's arm, and pointed. "What have you got there?"

"Oh, the Art Shop had the most lovely pink paper for me to make the badges and membership cards, but I had to get the whole roll." Daisy let Felicity peek inside the tube.

"Wow!" said Felicity, feeling all the better for seeing something pink. "It's really glittery."

"You could use what's left over to make a poster to get people to join," suggested Daisy. "Why don't you come back to my house now and we can work on our projects together?"

Feeling better, Felicity agreed and they flew off.

"What do you think?" said Felicity, holding up her poster when it was finally finished.

Fairies with Passion
are
Fairies of Fashion

WANTED

FASHIONABLE FAIRIES TO JOIN
FAIRY FASHION CLUB

Fairies wishing to join should
come to Sparkles café at
6pm tonight for an interview

"It looks lovely. With a poster like that I'm sure we'll get hundreds of fairies wanting to join." Daisy stood back and admired Felicity's poster.

"I'd better go and put it up," said Felicity looking at Daisy's clock. "We haven't long before we meet."

* * *

At 5pm Holly, Polly and Daisy sat at their favourite Sparkles Café table. Each wore a special Fashion Club uniform T-shirt designed by Holly, adorned with a perfectly matching Club Badge created by Daisy.

They were testing each other on the password and codes made up by Polly. Felicity was fashionably late!

"You won't believe what I've just seen outside!" panted Felicity as she sat down next to her friends. "There's a queue to join the Fairy Fashion Club that stretches all the way to Star Street!"

"I hope you found us big head-quarters!" said Holly.

Felicity gasped and put her hand over her mouth.

"Oh, I'm such a flop of a fairy!" she muffled through her fingers. "I was

47

so happy designing the poster to look fashionably beautiful, I forgot all about looking for headquarters. The most we can have is ten fairies, and that's only if I keep my bedroom tidy."

"Oh Felicity!" the fairy friends chorused.

"With the four of us that only leaves six fairies to choose from all of those waiting outside! It's going to be tough!" said Polly.

"We'd better begin!" said Holly.

Felicity ushered the first Fashion Club candidate in.

Tall fairies, slim fairies, loud fairies, small fairies, fairies they had never seen before, stood in front of the Fashion Club panel to say why

they thought they should be chosen
to join.

* * *

By the time the last fairy in the
queue had been interviewed it was
dark outside.

"They were all so nice!" said
Felicity. "If only every one of them
could join our Fashion Club."

Sparkles Café

"The one with the checked dress and stripy tights wasn't very fashionable," said Holly, looking down her list.

"Yes, but she was very good at needlework and had the prettiest shoes," said Felicity.

"Well, the fairy with the blue hair was a bit over the top for our club, I thought," said Polly.

"Well, I think it's nice to have a bit of a variety," replied Felicity.

"If only we had bigger club headquarters," said Daisy, twiddling with her rose hair grip. "Fairies and fashion are like flowers," she continued. "Flowers have their own scent and colour that make them individual, and each fairy has something that sets them apart from all the others... and together we make the most wonderful bouquet! Felicity's right, we can't leave anyone out."

"That's it!" squealed Felicity, pinging so far out of her seat her crown nearly bumped the ceiling.  "I've got it! Our Fashion Club headquarters should be somewhere filled with flowers, where we can all sit comfortably surrounded by colourful inspiration…"

Felicity paused and took a deep breath to continue.

"We should meet in Daisy's greenhouse!" she exclaimed. "If Daisy doesn't mind."

"I don't mind at all!" said Daisy.

"Perfect!" said Holly, who was already filling in the address on the membership cards.

"Just lovely," said Polly.

"I'll go and tell everyone!" said Felicity excitedly. She flew over to the other side of the café where the interviewees were anxiously waiting to see if they'd made the top ten.

"I'm afraid the number of successful applicants has changed," announced Felicity pretending to look sad. Forlorn fairy faces groaned and some reached for their coats. "We've decided to only have…" and Felicity tried hard to contain her giggles, "… ALL OF YOU!!" she burst out. Relieved fairies whooped with surprise as the most fashionable fairy cheer filled the café.

Designer Drama

Felicity Wishes had called an
emergency Fairy Fashion Club
meeting and was teetering on the
edge of one of Daisy's potting tables
clapping her hands for "Quiet!"

All the fairies from the School of Nine Wishes were on school holidays. As founder members, Felicity and her three best fairy friends, Holly, Polly and Daisy, were in charge of the club that was dedicated to all things fashionable.

"Quiet please," shouted Felicity again, clapping her hands louder.

The Fashion Club had been a brilliant success and over thirty chattering fairies were crammed into Daisy's greenhouse, officially known as "Fashion Club Headquarters".

Finally, a hush descended on the room.

"Fashion Fairies," said Felicity, a little nervous speaking to such a large group. "Thank you for coming to this emergency meeting at such short notice. As you know I have a special announcement to make."

All the fairies looked up at Felicity

expectantly.

"Stella Fluttiano, the world famous fashion designer, is coming to Bloomfield!"

Suddenly the room was full of excited fairy whispers and quivering fairy wings.

"She is giving a lecture on the new look for next season, which, as you know, is a closely guarded secret. Those attending the lecture will be the first to hear which fashionable colours will be the most magical for the coming year!"

The fairies couldn't contain themselves any longer, and suddenly the whole room was full of fairy squeals and chatter.

"Shhh, please!" said Felicity. "Quiet!" she pleaded, smiling.

"There are no tickets. Admission to the lecture will be on a first come, first served basis. This will mean some careful organisation. Polly has the details."

And with that Felicity fluttered down from the table as delicately as she could to allow Polly to take her place.

"Fashion Fairies," said Polly, more confidently than Felicity. " I have here a list, that I have photocopied for you all. It details a plan to ensure that we can all be the first to see the beautiful colours Stella Fluttiano has chosen to set the fashion trend for next season. We are going to camp overnight to make sure we are first in the queue."

And Polly waved a pink sheet of paper in the air high above her head so that all the fairies could see.

"If you'd like to come to me on your way out I'll give you a sheet, and if you could all read it through by next meeting we will be able put our plans in place. Thank you for attending this Fashion Club meeting at such short notice."

* * *

When all the club members had left and Daisy's greenhouse was finally empty, Felicity, Holly, Polly and Daisy wandered up to the house.

"Anyone for milkshake?" said Daisy producing a large box of plump red strawberries from her fridge.

"Yummy! Yes, please!" said Felicity.

"Silly question!" said Holly.

"Not for me, thanks," said Polly who was engrossed in scribbling notes in her Fashion Club meeting book.

"Are you sure we're up to organising a camping trip for thirty fairies?" said Felicity, peeping over her friend's shoulder as she wrote.

"It's the only way if we all want to see Stella Fluttiano," said Polly putting down her pen and looking up. "We'll have to get there at least the day before the lecture to start queuing to get in. I've heard fairies from as far away as Glitter Beach are coming to hear her talk."

"It will be such an adventure!" said Daisy excitedly as she put down the three milkshakes on the table and joined the others.

"You would say that!" said Holly, who did not share her friend's enthusiasm. "It's all right for you, you want to be a Blossom Fairy when you leave school. Camping in a field will be great experience for getting closer to nature."

Unlike her friend, Holly had no desire to "get close to nature" and wanted to be a Christmas Tree Fairy when she left the School of Nine Wishes. It was certainly not because she liked trees, but she guessed rightly that it would involve the least amount of effort and the maximum amount of admiration for her beautiful looks.

Holly swished her hair dramatically "But if being dedicated to fashion means making sacrifices, then this camping trip is one I'll just have to make."

"It won't be that bad," said Polly, handing everyone a pink sheet. "Have a read, it will be like a mini-holiday!"

The four fairy friends pored over the details Polly had carefully put

together to ensure they could all see Stella Fluttiano in action. The talk was to take place in a large marquee right in the middle of a field next to Blue Twinkle Lake. Polly had arranged to hire four large tents and each fairy was to bring her own sleeping bag, wash bag, pyjamas and towel.

* * *

At last the day came when all thirty Fashion Club fairies set off on their first club trip away. Bloomfield wasn't

far from Little Blossoming, which
was lucky as each fairy carried a
heavy bag. Flying straight when
weighed down with bags took an
awful lot of concentration!

When they finally arrived in the
field there were already dozens of
fairies flying around preparing for a
night in the queue leading up to the
grand marquee.

There was no time to lose. In order to secure their place at the front, it was important to get the tents up and in position as soon as possible. Being a friendly fairy, Felicity was put in charge of finding volunteers to help.

It wasn't long before she had a team of fairies eagerly awaiting instructions.

"The tents are over there," said Polly, pointing to a large pile of green waterproof cloth, "and the instructions are here." And she handed Felicity a small booklet.

Felicity opened it, looked at the pictures, closed it, and put on her best confident look. Felicity usually only used her confident look when she had absolutely no idea about what she was supposed to be doing.

"Right," she said. "If everyone takes a pile of these," Felicity pointed

to the tent pegs, "and if you divide
yourselves into groups of four and
take a tent each, I'll come round
and show you where to start."

A few hours later, Holly came
round to inspect the progress. "They
don't look very fashionable tents to
me," she said, prodding the orange
gauze with her wand.

Felicity frowned. "I tried to get the
tent walls tight, but these pegs are

just too bendy." She was secretly
happy that she'd been able to get the
tents up at all.

"They're not tent pegs, silly!" said
Holly, bursting out into fits of giggles.
"They're the skewers for the barbeque.
Polly's been looking for those for
ages!"

Holly could see Polly still
rummaging through bags on the
other side of the field and motioned
for her to come over. "I've found your
skewers," said Holly, pointing.

"Does that mean that I'll have to take all the tents down and start again?" said Felicity forlornly.

"I'm afraid you'd have to do that even if you had used the proper tent pegs," said Daisy. "These tents are inside out. They're supposed to be orange on the inside, and green on the outside!"

Felicity's wings drooped.

Seeing her friend's despair, Holly said, "Don't worry, I'll help your team to turn them the right way round."

* * *

By nightfall all the fashionably green tents were up, and thirty fairies were full to the brim with delicious barbeque food. Sleepily they each took it in turns to go down to the lake to wash and brush their teeth, and before the moon was high in the sky everyone was fast asleep.

Everyone except for Felicity, who was too excited to do anything except think of the colour combinations that might be forecast by Stella Fluttiano tomorrow.

Peeping outside the tent door into the night air, Felicity could just about make out the marquee that fairies were still putting up. As she yawned, Felicity remembered that she hadn't

yet brushed her teeth, and by torch light she tiptoed down to the lake's edge. By the time she was ready to head back, her eyes had grown so accustomed to the dark that she found her way by the light of the moon.

When Felicity snuggled back into bed she found it a lot more cosy and warm than she had left it, and as she

cuddled her toy rabbit it felt a lot bigger than it usually did.

It was only when she gave her soft toy an extra loving squeeze that it made a squeak, which woke Felicity up with a start. Her rabbit had never squeaked before! Scrambling for her torch, Felicity turned it on, only to get a shock that made her jump with fright.

"What are you doing in my tent?" squealed a fairy Felicity had never seen before.

Waving her torch with confusion, Felicity frantically flew towards the door.

"Sorry," she spluttered. "I must have got mixed up!"

The shock of finding herself in another fairy's tent, had woken her up completely and Felicity stood wide-eyed looking into the semi-darkness.

The grand marquee looked magnificent; it was finally up and finished. Felicity rubbed her eyes. It looked like it was moving.

"Surely not," whispered Felicity to herself. "Maybe I'm just dreaming."

But as her eyes grew more accustomed to the dark, she could make out that the edge of the marquee was definitely moving

towards the far end of the field.
Curious, Felicity went to investigate.

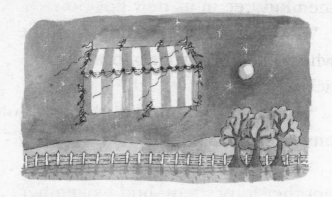

As she neared the marquee she
could see that dozens of working
fairies were flying it slowly away
from its original position.

"What's happening?" said Felicity
to one of the security fairies standing
close by.

"Oh, we're moving it. There's
supposed to be brilliant sunshine
tomorrow, and if we keep the
marquee where it is everyone inside
will get too hot. There's a spot over
here," said the fairy, "that is shaded

by trees, which will be much better."

Felicity watched the fairies settle the marquee in its new position.

"But that will mean that everyone who was at the front of the queue will now be at the back."

"Hmm," said the security fairy. "Not ideal, I know, but it can't be helped."

GRAND MARQEE

GRAND MARQUEE

"But you don't understand, I'm here with thirty very good friends, and we've spent so much hard work preparing for this trip. We've all been looking forward to seeing Stella Fluttiano for so long, everyone's going to be very upset. Now we'll be at the back of the queue and won't get in."

"Yes, I'm sure you and your friends won't be the only ones," said the security fairy unhelpfully. "You could always save them a place in the new queue, but it will mean sleeping here all night. If you stay now you'll be the first. Other fairies camping won't discover the queue's moved until sunrise when they wake up."

Felicity hadn't stopped to hear the end of the security fairy's sentence. She had already flown back to her tent, grabbed a sleeping bag and was positioned right at the front of

the new entrance. Even the thought
of the creepy-crawlies and the dark
didn't put her off.

* * *

Felicity woke the next morning to
excited squeals coming from Polly,
Daisy and Holly.

"Thank goodness," they cried,
showering her with hugs.

"We thought you'd got lost!" said
Polly.

"The whole of the Fairy
Fashion Club has
been looking for
you everywhere!"
said Daisy.

"What a wonderful surprise to find you not only safe, but at the front of the new queue!" said Holly, full of admiration.

GRAND MARQUEE

"Anything for my friends!" said Felicity, stretching and admiring the rosy glow of the sunrise. "I wonder what colour Stella will have us all wearing next season. I hope it's pink!"

If you enjoyed this book, why not try another of these fantastic story collections?

Clutter Clean-out

Designer Drama

Newspaper Nerves

Star Surprise

Emma Thomson's

felicity Wishes®

Designer Drama

and other stories

Hodder
Children's
Books

A division of Hodder Headline Limited